S0-CJP-119

The Phantom of Creepy Hollow

A Mummy Dearest Creepy Hollow WhoooooooooDunnit?

By Robert Kraus

WARNER JUVENILE BOOKS
A Time Warner Company
New York

Warner Juvenile Books Edition
Copyright © 1988 by Robert Kraus
All rights reserved.

Warner Books, Inc., 666 Fifth Avenue, New York, NY 10103
A Time Warner Company

Printed in the United States of America
First Warner Juvenile Books Printing: October 1988
10 9 8 7 6 5 4 3 2

Library of Congress Cataloging-in-Publication Data

Kraus, Robert
The phantom of Creepy Hollow.

"A Mummy dearest Creepy Hollow whoooooooodunnit?"
Summary: Mummy succeeds in cornering the Phantom of the Opry and revealing his secret identity.
[1. Monsters—Fiction. 2. Humorous stories]
I. Title.
PZ7.K868Pc 1988 [E] 87-40698
ISBN 1-55782-060-0

Here's a Tale
To Make You Shudder
About A Mummy
And Not
Your Mudder!
The Teller of Tales
INK

It is opening night and all the Creeps are going to the Opry.

I SMELL TROUBLE.
HOW ABOUT A BITE AFTER THE SHOW, BABY?
OPRY HOUSE
KEEP YOUR FANGS TO YOUR-SELF.
TONITE
WEIRDO'S
MONSTER
BASH
LIP-SMACKIN' GOOD!

SHHHH, NOAH. LET ME ENJOY THE MOOSIC.
THOSE BUBBLES MEAN TROUBLE, MUMMY.
POP CORN

The Phantom of the Opry has put bubble bath in the brass section!

Pop
Corn

IS THERE A DETECTIVE IN THE HOUSE?

I'VE CHAN
INTO A BAT,
POP
CORN

THE BUBBLE FOOTPRINTS WILL LEAD US TO THE CULPRIT!

COME INTO MY PARLOR, LI'L FLY.
NO WAY
I'M RIGHT BEHIND YOU, MUMMY.
FOOT-PRINTS DON'T FIB.
WHAT TH-

DUM DEE DUM
CREEPY SONATA
ZZZZZ

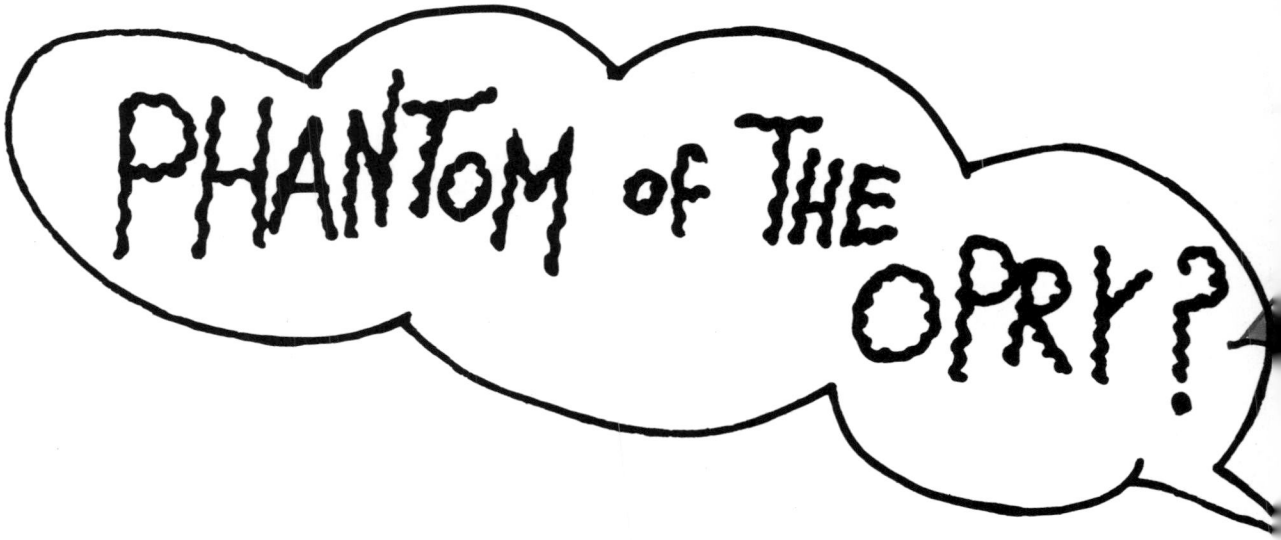

The Phantom presses a secret button and…

WHO ELSE?
WHY THE MASK, BOOBY? YOU UGLY OR SOMETHING?
I'M HIDEOUS.
CREEPY HOLLOW RAG

Mummy and Noah fall into the
open jaws of hungry alligators.

Is this the end of Mummy Dearest?

Is this the end of Noah Count?

Is this the end of the story?

INCLUDE ME OUT!
JUST WHEN I THOUGHT IT WAS SAFE TO GO BACK IN THE WATER!
I WANT MUM IN MY TUM!
YUMMY YUMMY I LOVE MUMMY.

"Don't snap at me!" snaps Mummy.
She takes out her gator aid kit
and tapes up the gators' jaws.

UGH!
MUZZLE!
GLUMP!

Mummy rides a gator to freedom.

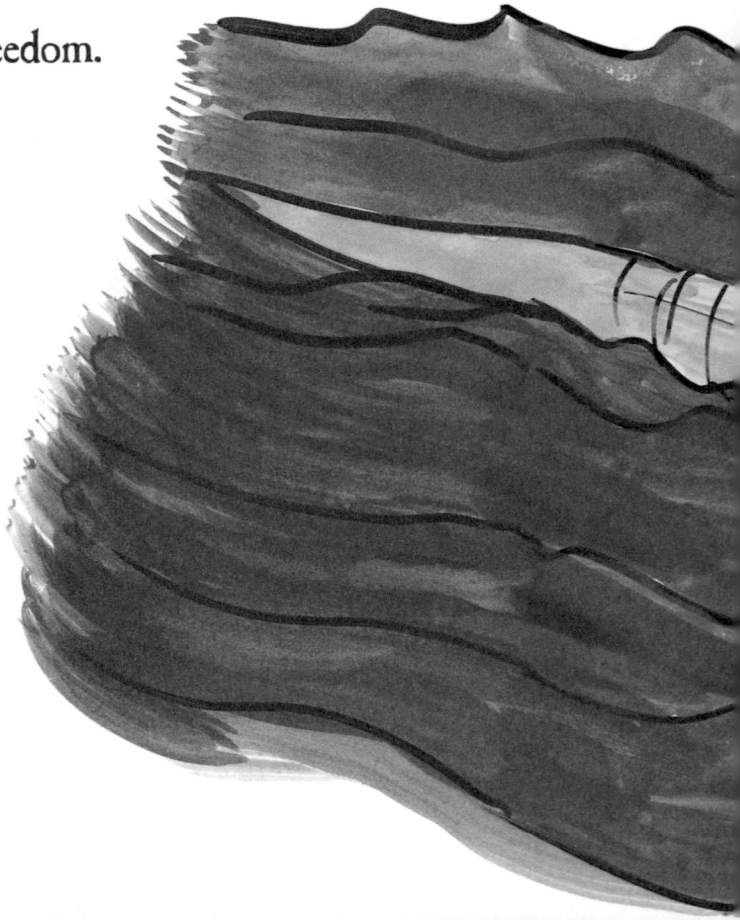

HI YO, ALLIGATOR, AWAY!
EXIT

I'LL BURN HIM!
NEVER FEAR, MUMMY'S HERE!
I'LL SMASH HIM!
I'LL LEARN HIM!

Meanwhile, an angry mob pursues the Phantom.

THE PHANTOM SHALL NOT ESCAPE!
YEA!
I'LL CLUB HIM!
I'LL DRUB HIM!

The Phantom hides in a garbage can and eludes the bloodthirsty mob.

Mummy, great detective that she is,
spots the Phantom peeking out of the garbage can.

COME OUT, PHANTOM, THE JIG IS UP!
OH, DEAR.

Whoooooooo is the Phantom of Creepy Hollow?

Evil Dentist II?
A real pain in the molar.

Tina Lizzy?
Alias Lotta Hair
A girl after
my own hea

Boney Goodman?
Did he swing it?

Norman, the man-eating plant?
A real late bloomer.

Everybody's favorite,
Mister Monster?

The Ol' Perfessor?
Always a little suspect.

Name withheld,
winner of the best mustache
and goatee contest?

What's your guess?
It's as good as mine.

It's MISTER MONSTER!

PRACTICE.
I WON'T TURN YOU IN IF YOU PROMISE TO PRACTICE EVERY DAY, BIG GUY.
I PROMISE, I PROMISE. AND THANKS, MUMMY.
WHAT ARE MUMMYS FOR?

GOOD MONSTER.
THANKS, MUMMY.
INK
Practice makes Perfect
The Teller of Tales